Hairy Maclary's SHOWBUSINESS

Lynley Dodd

PUFFIN

In Riverside Hall
on Cabbage Tree Row,
the Cat Club were having
their Annual Show.

There were fat cats
and thin cats,
tabbies and greys,
kick-up-a-din cats
with boisterous ways.
Cooped up in cages,
they practised their wails
while their owners fussed over
their teeth
and their
tails.

Out in the street,
tied to a tree,
Hairy Maclary
was trying to see.
He struggled and squirmed,
he unravelled the knot
and dragging his lead,
he was off
at the
trot.

He bounced up the steps,
he pounced through the door,
he pricked up his ears
and he pranced round the floor;
flapping and flustering,
bothering,
blustering,
leaving behind him
a hiss
and a
roar.

'STOP!'
cried the President,
'COLLAR HIM, QUICK!'
But Hairy Maclary
was slippery slick.

He slid under tables,

he jumped over chairs,

he skittered through legs

and he sped down the stairs.

In and out doorways,
through banners and flags,

tangling together
belongings and bags.

Along came Miss Plum
with a big silver cup.
'GOT HIM!' she said
as she snaffled him up.

Preening and purring,
the prizewinners sat
with their rosettes and cups
on the prizewinners' mat...

and WHO
won the prize
for the SCRUFFIEST CAT?

Hairy Maclary
from Donaldson's Dairy.

PUFFIN BOOKS

Published by the Penguin Group: London, New York, Australia, Canada, India, Ireland, New Zealand and South Africa

Penguin Books Ltd, Registered Offices: 80 Strand, London WC2R 0RL, England

puffinbooks.com

First published in New Zealand by Mallinson Rendel Publishers Ltd 1991
First published in Great Britain in Puffin Books 1993
Reissued in 2005
051
Text and illustrations copyright © Lynley Dodd, 1991
Made and printed in China
ISBN: 978–0–140–54550–0